HEROES OF HOPE

22 INSPIRING STORIES OF CHRISTIANS FROM AROUND THE WORLD

SHARON PRENTIS
AND
ALYSIA-LARA AYONRINDE

Text copyright © 2025 Sharon Prentis and Alysia-Lara Ayonrinde
Illustrations by Amanda Quartey, Amanda Yoshida, Ana Latese,
Anastasia Magloire Williams, Ashley Evans, Daniela Gamba, David Wilkerson,
Jen Khatun, Neda Kazemifar, Richy Sanchez Ayala and Samya Zitouni
This edition copyright © 2025 The Society for Promoting Christian Knowledge

Published by **Starshine Books**
Part of the SPCK Group
The Record Hall
16–16A Baldwin's Gardens
London
EC1N 7RJ
www.spck.org.uk

ISBN 978-1-91574-930-7

Acknowledgements
Frame illustrations © Getty Images

First edition 2025

A catalogue record for this book is available from the British Library

Produced on paper from sustainable sources

10 9 8 7 6 5 4 3 2 1

Printed and bound in the Hong Kong by Dream Colour Printing Ltd
Typeset by SPCK

CONTENTS

FOREWORD BY LORD PAUL BOATENG

INTRODUCTION

6   ST MAURICE: A BRAVE SOLDIER OF FAITH

10   ABBA MOSES: A STORY OF CHANGE AND FORGIVENESS

14   ST MONICA: THE PATRON SAINT OF MOTHERS

18   ST AUGUSTINE OF HIPPO: THE SEARCH FOR UNDERSTANDING

22   ST JUAN DIEGO CUAUHTLATOATZIN: A MAN WHO DARED TO BELIEVE

26   ST MARTIN DE PORRES: A HEART FOR CHARITY

30   ST KATERI TEKAKWITHA: THE 'LILY OF THE MOHAWKS'

34   ST KURIAKOSE ELIAS CHAVARA: A PIONEER OF FREE EDUCATION

38   PAULINA DLAMINI: A FAITH INFLUENCER

42   BLESSED CEREFINO GIMINÉZ MALLA: THE STRONG ONE

46   ST JOSEPHINE BAKHITA: A TALE OF TRIUMPH OVER ADVERSITY

50   DR HAROLD MOODY: A BEACON OF UNITY AND COMPASSION

54   TOYOHIKO KAGAWA: A PEACEMAKER AND COMMUNITY BUILDER

58   TSAI 'CHRISTIANA' SU JUAN: THE QUEEN OF THE DARK CHAMBER

62   INI KOPURIA: A PIONEER BRIDGING FAITH AND CULTURE

66   FLORENCE LI TIM-OI: THE FIRST FEMALE ANGLICAN PRIEST

70   OSEOLA MCCARTY: A SELFLESS GIFT OF GENEROSITY

74   ST ALPHONSA: A LIFE OF SACRIFICE FOR OTHERS

78   PAULI MURRAY: A CIVIL RIGHTS ACTIVIST

82   ROSA PARKS: A WOMAN WHO REFUSED TO MOVE

86   ARCHBISHOP OSCAR ROMERO: A VOICE FOR JUSTICE

90   ARCHBISHOP DESMOND TUTU: A CHAMPION OF HOPE

GLOSSARY AND ILLUSTRATORS

FOREWORD

LORD PAUL BOATENG

Many years ago, when I was a child in Africa, my grandfather built the church in the village where I was baptized. He did not have an easy time building the church; some people tried to stop him. But he never gave up, because he loved Jesus, and he knew Jesus loved him.

I wish that when I was growing up I had a wonderful book like this one, with stories of how women and men from many different lands and backgrounds did great things because Jesus told them to love the world just as he loved them.

I was lucky, though, to have the example of my grandfather and my parents who gave up a lot to help build a new country: Ghana. They too were made strong by a loving Jesus.

I have tried in my life, which I have lived in both Britain and Africa, to make a difference so that I and other people could live full and happy lives. Life has not always been easy. Bad stuff sometimes happens, but Jesus has always been there for me.

I know Jesus wants the best for us all and loves each one of us. He made us all differently, but we are all members of one family. He wants us to love and take care of one another and this wonderful planet Earth and every living thing on it.

The men and women in this book knew that. They lived and worked and gave up much, including sometimes their own lives, so that the world could be better.

I was lucky enough to know one of them: Archbishop Desmond Tutu. I worked with and for him, and long before that was inspired by his example. He did many great things. But I remember him also as a man who loved to laugh and dance, and who could never get enough of the homemade rum-and-raisin ice cream my wife Janet made especially for him.

Archbishop Desmond and all the people in this book were young once, and, at some point as they grew up, they came to know Jesus. They were individuals just like you and me, but Jesus helped them do very special things that changed their lives and other people's lives, and made the world a better place.

Jesus can do the same for each of you reading this book. So, enjoy reading about these special people. I pray that you too may lead happy and useful lives.

Paul

The Rt Hon the Lord Boateng CVO:
Paul was born in Britain but moved to Ghana with his family at the age of four. As a teenager, he was forced to flee Ghana and move back to Britain with his mother and his sister. After school and university, he worked as a lawyer. In 2002, he became the first Black Cabinet Minister (one of the most senior people in the British government). In 2005, he became the first Black ambassador in British history. He is a Methodist lay preacher.

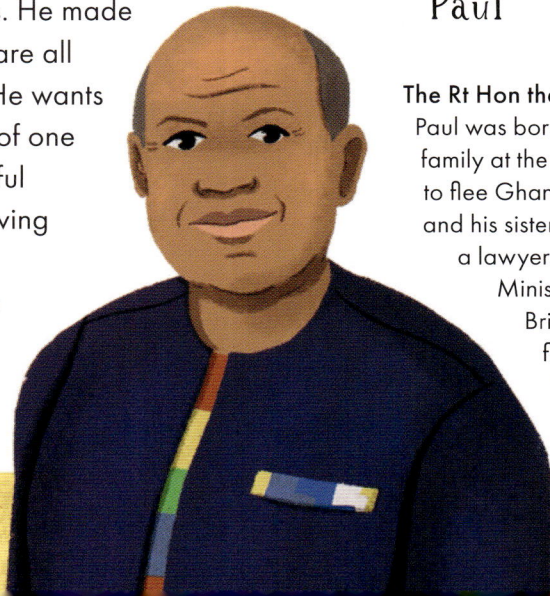

INTRODUCTION

Dear Reader,

Welcome to a world of inspiration! In this book, you will meet 22 incredible people from around the world. Their stories tell of bravery and courage through difficult times. These individuals came from different backgrounds and cultures, but they all shared one thing in common: their strong Christian faith. Each one believed in something greater than themselves, and this led to a desire to help others. But they didn't just dream about improving the lives of other people; they got on and did it!

You may not have heard of many of these extraordinary people before, but that's what makes their stories even more special. From the cities of Europe to the deserts of Africa, from the wild open spaces of America to the busy streets of China and the green, tropical beauty of the Solomon Islands, each person featured in this book has made a difference in their local communities in their own unique way, all because of their faith and determination.

As you read each story, take a moment to reflect on the challenges these individuals faced and how they overcame them with the help of their faith. Think about the questions at the end of each story: What would you have done in their shoes? How can their actions inspire you to make a difference in your own community?

Don't keep these thoughts to yourself! Instead, share them with your friends, family, and teachers. Discussing these stories with others could help you gain new insights that you may not have considered before.

So, get ready to be inspired by the amazing stories of these 22 individuals who have left a lasting impact on the world. We hope their stories ignite a spark within you to make a difference, whether big or small. Let's begin this journey and discover the power of faith and determination...

Sharon and Alysia-Lara

Illustrator: Amanda Quartey

ST MAURICE

A BRAVE SOLDIER OF FAITH

Do you know someone who stood up for what they believed in, even when it might have been difficult? Well, back in the third century a Roman solider called Maurice did just that. He was a man known for his courage and faith not only during battle, but also when he had to make a choice either to follow a decision and obey a cruel Roman emperor, or go against him and die.

Maurice was born in Thebes, Egypt, around AD 250. He joined the Roman army, becoming a soldier in the powerful Roman Empire. What made Maurice different was that he was a Christian, a follower of Jesus Christ, which was not a widely accepted faith among Romans at that time.

Unlike many other officers, he treated his soldiers with kindness and respect. As a result, many of them became Christians too. The other commanders worshipped the Roman deities, or gods. In fact, the Roman emperor Maximus, who ruled at the time, saw Christianity as a threat to his authority, making it extremely difficult for Christians like Maurice to serve in the military.

Emperor Maximus decided to send Maurice and his men to Gaul (a large

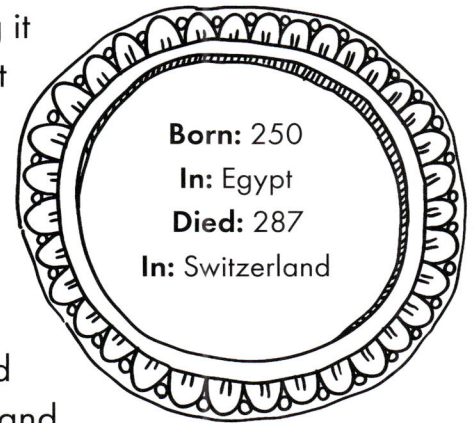

Born: 250
In: Egypt
Died: 287
In: Switzerland

area that now covers Belgium, Germany, France, Luxembourg, the Netherlands, and parts of Switzerland and northern Italy), to suppress and stop a rebellion. Before going into battle, it was usual for soldiers to offer sacrifices to the Roman gods and promise their loyalty to the emperor. However, Maurice, as a follower of Jesus Christ, refused to worship the Roman gods. He believed that his loyalty belonged only to God and not to the emperor.

When he was ordered to worship the emperor, Maurice refused! His heart was determined and he would not change his mind, even knowing he would face severe consequences.

When the emperor learned of Maurice's defiance, he ordered that one in every ten of Maurice's men should be killed, a punishment known as "decimation." Despite the threat, Maurice and his men stood firm in their faith and refused to deny their beliefs. In a desperate attempt to force them to obey, the emperor ordered another hundred men to be killed, but Maurice and his soldiers remained determined. The emperor was increasingly angered by their refusal to submit to him. He made a drastic decision. He ordered that the entire regiment, including Maurice, were to be executed for disobeying orders. Maurice remained firm in his faith, choosing to be true to his belief in God even in the face of death.

There is also another version of this story, which has Maurice refusing to kill other Christians in battle. This suggests an alternative reason for Maurice and his men being killed or martyred for their faith.

Many paintings

show Maurice as a Black soldier, making him the first person of African heritage to be represented in European medieval art. Historical records about Maurice are scarce, with some even suggesting that parts of his story might be made up. However, places like Saint Maurice-en-Valais in Switzerland and an abbey in Magdeburg, Germany, which are dedicated to him, are proof of his importance.

Saint Maurice's story is one of bravery and unwavering faith. He stood up for his beliefs, even when it meant facing persecution and death. His courage and commitment to his faith have inspired many people over the centuries, reminding us of the importance of staying true to what is right, no matter the challenges we face.

QUESTIONS TO CONSIDER

1. Why do you think Saint Maurice chose to remain loyal to his faith, even when faced with death?

2. How can Saint Maurice's story inspire us to stand up for what we believe in, even when it's difficult?

3. Think of a time when you showed great courage. Write about it and share the story with family and friends.

ABBA MOSES

A STORY OF CHANGE AND FORGIVENESS

Born: 330
In: Egypt
Died: 405
In: Egypt

Have you ever wondered whether people can really change? Well, they can. Often, it is because something dramatic has happened to them. The story of Abba Moses is about someone who made a remarkable change from a man who didn't care about people to one who loved them.

Moses, who would later become known as Abba (or "Father") Moses, was born into slavery in Egypt in the year 330. He was tall and very strong, and because of that, he was chosen to work in the house of an important Egyptian official who owned him. However, he was also a thief. Soon his owner tired of Moses' dishonesty and threw him out of the house.

Angry and upset at everyone, Moses joined a group of thieves, quickly becoming their leader. Together they would roam the desert stealing from

anyone they came across. The group caused such havoc and mayhem that people feared Moses and his men.

One day, while trying to find a place to hide after a robbery, Moses stumbled upon a monastery at a city called Petra. He wanted to keep away from everyone until things quietened down and people stopped looking for him. Day after day he watched the monks who lived there carry on with their prayers. At first, the monks were afraid of him and wanted

to avoid him, but after a while, they decided to be kind to him. They shared their food and did not hand him in to the authorities. They started telling Moses about Jesus and how God loved him.

This was the first time Moses had ever heard such things. He was struck by how different the monks were from other people. Moses decided he wanted to become a better person and follow Jesus like the monks at the monastery and the hermits who lived away from society.

At first, the monks were doubtful that someone like Moses, who had done bad things, could truly change. However, Moses worked hard to prove to himself that he had changed and could now be trusted to do the right thing. He prayed, lived a simple life, and helped the older monks.

Gradually, everybody saw that he had left his old ways and was trying his best to do good. One evening, when robbers tried to attack him, Moses challenged them about their actions and forgave them, surprising everyone. Inspired by his kindness, the robbers decided they, too, would change their ways and become monks.

Abba Moses continued his life of prayer and solitude for many years. On occasions he would teach others about what it meant to follow Jesus Christ and become a better person.

Eventually, he became the head, or abbot, of his monastery. As he grew old, Abba Moses became well respected and loved by many.

One day, Abba Moses came across two menacing-looking men. As they inched closer and closer to him, shouting and prodding him, it was clear they wanted to fight. However, instead of

feeling scared, Abba Moses, with great courage, gently turned towards them and calmly said, "I will not fight you." The angry men came even closer, so close that Abba Moses could feel their hot breaths on his face. Despite the danger, he repeated calmly, with a strong voice and a gentle smile, "I choose peace because even when people decide to hurt, I will love." The men stood still for a moment, shocked by Abba Moses' approach.

His life of forgiveness and transformation is remembered by many. He taught that having a pure heart and remembering God's love are the most important things in life. Abba Moses' legacy shows us that with God's help, anyone can change for the better and make a difference by inspiring kindness, forgiveness, and good actions in others.

QUESTIONS TO CONSIDER

1. What made Abba Moses change after meeting the monks at the monastery?

2. Can you think of a time when someone's kindness helped you to change your mind? How did it make you feel?

3. What important lessons does Abba Moses' life teach us about making a difference in the world?

Illustrator: Anastasia Magloire Williams

ST MONICA

THE PATRON SAINT OF MOTHERS

Born: 331
In: Algeria
Died: 387
In: Italy

Have you ever had a family member worry about you, or whom you are worried about? You may even pray for them, hoping that they will be OK. Perhaps it's a younger brother or sister, or a parent. Well, you are not alone. Saint Monica, a woman from North Africa, had a son named Augustine who caused her a lot of worry. But through her love, patience, and unwavering and determined faith, she never gave up on him. He grew up to be one of the most important Christian thinkers and leaders of his time.

Monica was born in Algeria around the year 331. She belonged to the Berber, also known as the Amazigh, tribe. She was a loving and sensitive girl who grew up in a Roman city called Thagaste. She became a Christian as a teenager, but soon after her parents gave her away to a man called Patritius to be married.

When Monica married, she faced many challenges. Her husband did not share her faith, and at times he argued with Monica, making her very unhappy. Their son Augustine also did not follow his mother's faith and got into a lot of trouble in his younger years. Sometimes he did not come home for days. Monica worried about his future, and she often cried over his actions. As he grew older,

Augustine felt that he needed to leave home to study and find out more about the world. Although she would miss her son, Monica sadly agreed. She believed in his potential and wanted to support him, never giving up on him. Monica continued to pray for Augustine's well-being, showing her firm love and patience as a mother.

Monica's prayers and persistence eventually paid off. Through Monica's love and prayers, Augustine finally became a Christian and found peace in his faith. He now understood what Monica had meant all along by God's forgiving and endless love.

Monica was overjoyed, because for many years her son did not want to know about God. Augustine later wrote about the impact Monica had on his life in his famous book *Confessions*. He described Monica's quiet persistence, and he said that she "had planted the seeds of faith" in his heart, leading him to follow in her footsteps.

As Augustine's faith grew, he and Monica journeyed to Rome and Milan together. Monica's wisdom and faith led Augustine to invite her to debate with his friends, and she gave many wise answers. Sadly, on their way back to North Africa, Monica fell ill and passed away.

Augustine was deeply affected by his mother's death and wrote

about her difficult life and firm and determined faith. Monica's impact on Augustine was to encourage him to know God for himself. She recognized that the questions he had came from a desire to know that there was something bigger to believe in.

Monica was canonized, or made a saint, in the 390s, and is today recognized as the patron saint of mothers. Her story teaches us the importance of never giving up on our loved ones and of the power of prayer. Just like Saint Monica, we can show love, patience, and faith towards those who may need guidance and support.

QUESTIONS TO CONSIDER

1. Have you ever had a family member or friend who needed your support and prayers? How did you show them you cared?

2. What do you think it means to have "unwavering" faith like Saint Monica? How can you apply this in your own life?

3. Write a list of family members or friends who are having a difficult time. You don't need to write anything by their names, but trust that God knows them. As you write, think of them with love and thank God for them.

Illustrator: Daniela Gamba

ST AUGUSTINE OF HIPPO

THE SEARCH FOR UNDERSTANDING

Have you ever wondered about some of the big questions in life, such as what is good and evil, or how do we find truth and purpose? These are some of the things that Saint Augustine, a great scholar and Christian, explored in his writings and teachings.

Augustine was born in a busy North African town called Thagaste nearly 2,000 years ago, a place bustling with people from different cultures from across the Roman Empire. He lived there with his family, who belonged to the Berber, also known as the Amazigh, tribe. Although his family was not wealthy, they had everything they needed. His father, Patricius Aurelius, was a respected town councillor. He was a pagan with no religious beliefs who enjoyed the best things in life, such as tasty food and fine wine. Augustine's mother, Monica, was a devout Christian who showed a huge amount of patience with the way Patricius behaved.

Born: 354
In: Algeria
Died: 430
In: Algeria

As Augustine grew up, he rebelled against his mother's faith and embraced the pagan lifestyle of his father. Despite his brilliance as a student, he found studying boring and often got into trouble. One day, aged 16, he stole pears from the orchard next door during the night, not to eat them but to smash them, just because he could. What

a terrible waste! His mother despaired over her son's antics and spent many nights worrying about. However, Augustine excelled in the skill of speaking in public debate, known as rhetoric.

At the age of 17, Augustine went to Carthage to further his studies. There, he partied, had a fun time, and ignored the advice of his mother to focus on his education. In this exciting place, despite having everything he ever wanted, Augustine felt lonely and sad! "Is this it?" he asked himself. Something inside him made him yearn for more in life. He decided to try to find out more about what was missing.

After completing his studies, Augustine became a teacher, exploring different religions. His search for truth led him to ask questions, and eventually, at age 31, he turned to Christianity. One day, he suddenly understood that everything he had been searching for did not bring him the hope he craved. Sitting in his garden, he heard a child's voice say, "Take up and read." Augustine knew the voice was from God and concerned the Bible. So, picking up a nearby scroll, he started to read a passage from a letter written by Saint Paul. What was written made him think deeply and touched his heart. He realized that the Jesus he was reading about was a real person.

Through his honesty, wisdom, and unceasing search for meaning, Augustine found comfort in the Christian faith and began to explore the teachings of Christ. He was also able to share his experiences with others so that they too could understand how to make the right choices. Many people came to seek his advice, and he became known for his wisdom and teaching of the Christian faith.

Augustine's journey to faith was not an easy one. He grappled with lots of questions about human nature, free will, and the existence of evil. During this time he wrote his famous book called *Confessions*, which reflected his thoughts about these questions. As Augustine delved deeper into his faith, he realized the importance of God's love and the need for the choices people make to reflect that love.

When he was older, Augustine became bishop of the city of Hippo at a time when the Roman Empire was starting to fall apart. He was popular because he encouraged the people through his words, helping them to remember that although there was chaos around them, they belonged to God's everlasting kingdom.

Through his courage, honesty, and persistent search for truth, Augustine inspires us to explore our own beliefs and question the world around us. His journey to understanding and faith is a reminder that life is often filled with challenges and lots of self-reflection but eventually we can find peace.

QUESTIONS TO CONSIDER

1. As a child Saint Augustine found it difficult to follow the faith of his mother. How did his upbringing shape his beliefs and worldview?

2. What struggles did Augustine face in his search for meaning and fulfilment?

3. How does Augustine's story inspire you to explore your own beliefs and values?

Illustrator: Daniela Gamba

ST JUAN DIEGO CUAUHTLATOATZIN
A MAN WHO DARED TO BELIEVE

Do you believe in miracles? A miracle is something extraordinary that cannot be explained by the rules of science or nature. Throughout history, the church has recognized certain events as divine miracles, meaning that they can only be explained as being caused by the power of God. Juan Diego witnessed one such miracle in Mexico. His story is a powerful example of how one person's devotion to God can create a lasting impact on many.

Juan Diego Cuauhtlatoatzin (his name means "Talking Eagle") grew up as a kind and humble farmer who was proud of his Aztec heritage. Born in 1474, Juan Diego loved his village, its people, and had deep faith in God.

One day Juan had an extraordinary experience. As he was walking along the winding, hilly road on his way to church, something caught his eye. He looked up. At the top of the hill, he saw something bright and glowing. He approached and saw a woman surrounded by light. It was the Virgin Mary!

Lovingly, she spoke to Juan and made a special request. She wanted him to ask the local bishop to build a church dedicated to her on that hill.

Born: 1474
In: Mexico
Died: 1548
In: Mexico

Excited and nervous, Juan Diego went to see the bishop. He explained what he had seen, but the bishop shook his head. He did not believe him. The bishop asked for a sign to prove that what Juan said was true. Determined to help his community, Juan returned to the hill, where the Virgin Mary appeared to him again. This time, she instructed Juan to gather flowers from the top of the hill. It was winter, not the usual time for blossoming flowers. Yet, Juan followed her instructions.

When he reached the top of the hill, he was amazed to find beautiful roses blooming there. He collected the roses in his tilma, the name for a traditional cloak worn in Mexico that could be used to carry things, and took them to the bishop. When Juan unfolded his tilma before the bishop, a miraculous image appeared on it: the image of the Virgin Mary, just as she had appeared to him! This extraordinary miracle convinced the bishop to believe Juan, and he agreed to build the church. The church, known as the Basilica of Our Lady of Guadalupe, became a significant place of worship and a symbol of faith for the community.

After the church was built, Juan Diego continued to share the story of the Virgin Mary's visit with others. His faith and dedication inspired many people and helped strengthen their sense of community. His story

encouraged people to come together in worship and support each other.

In 2002, in a ceremony at the Basilica of Guadelupe in Mexico, Pope John Paul II officially declared Juan Diego a saint. He was the first Indigenous (Native) person in Latin America to reach sainthood. His life is a great example of how faith and dedication to God can lead to positive change in a community.

QUESTIONS TO CONSIDER

1. How did Saint Juan Diego's actions help his community, and what was the result of his efforts?

2. Have you ever felt like you were part of something bigger than yourself? What does the story of the miraculous roses teach us about believing in something greater than ourselves?

3. How can you use your particular skills and beliefs to help make a positive impact in your community?

Illustrator: David Wilkerson

ST MARTIN DE PORRES

A HEART FOR CHARITY

Have you ever donated food to a foodbank, or helped those in need? The story of Martin de Porres challenges all of us to consider those who are less fortunate or struggling with ill health. It even challenges us to consider the welfare of animals. What would the world be like if we always put other people's needs before our own?

Born: 1579
In: Peru
Died: 1639
In: Peru

In the busy city of Lima, Peru, there lived a remarkable young boy named Martin de Porres. Born in 1579, Martin was known for his kind heart and his strong sense of justice. His father was from Spanish nobility and his mother was a freed enslaved woman of African and Indigenous descent. This mixed heritage sometimes made life hard for Martin because of the unkind and unfair prejudices of his time.

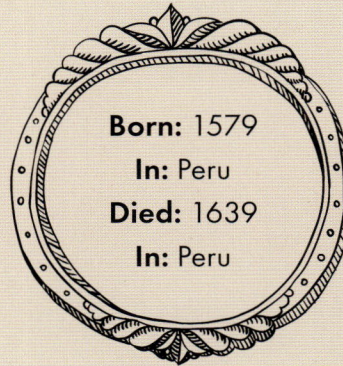

The family were extremely poor, and his mother could not afford to look after him. Martin went to school for only two years before, age 12, he left to work as an apprentice barber, also known as a junior surgeon, to help the family. From an early age, Martin was prayerful and showed a special kindness towards everyone around him. His deep Christian faith guided him. After his apprenticeship he decided to join the

Dominican Order, a group of people who dedicated their lives to serving God and helping others.

Martin had a unique gift. It was said that he could communicate with animals. People believed he could understand and even heal them. This special talent made him a friend to all creatures, no matter how big or small. He took care of animals with great love and respect, showing that every living being deserves compassion.

One significant moment in Martin's life came when a serious illness swept through the monastery where he lived. Many people were too scared to help those who were sick because they were afraid of catching the illness. But Martin stepped up courageously. He used his knowledge of herbal medicine, treatments made from plants and herbs, to help people feel better. This, along with his deep compassion to care for those who were suffering, enabled him to heal many people. His selfless actions helped people who were sick to recover and showed the importance of caring for others, even in tough times.

Martin also made an enormous impact through his work with the local community. At a time when the care of children was not a priority and many experienced cruelty and hardship, he established an orphanage and children's hospital. Other efforts included organizing a special charity kitchen to feed the hungry and provide meals for those in need. His efforts in running the charity kitchen showed his dedication to social justice and his desire to help everyone, especially those who were less fortunate. Social justice means making sure everyone is treated fairly and given the same chances to succeed, no matter their background. It is about ensuring that resources and opportunities

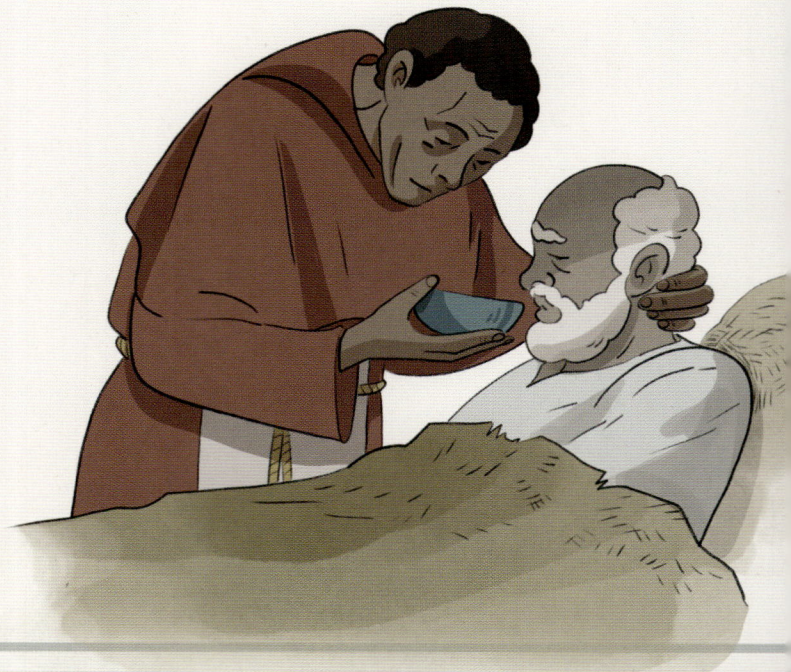

are shared equally and that everyone is treated with respect and kindness. Martin's dedication to helping others earned him the loving nickname "Martin of Charity." He was made a saint in 1962.

Saint Martin de Porres is remembered today as the patron saint of social justice, racial harmony, and people who have mixed heritage. His life teaches us that compassion and fairness can make a big difference. Even though he faced difficulties, he remained dedicated to helping others and working towards a better, more inclusive world.

QUESTIONS TO CONSIDER

1. How did Saint Martin de Porres use his unique gifts to help others, and how can you use your own talents to make a positive difference in your community?

2. Why do you think Martin chose to help people who were sick even when others were afraid, and how can you show bravery in your own actions to help others?

3. Think about the special connection Saint Martin de Porres had with animals. What animals do you feel connected to, and how can you show them kindness? Share your thoughts on creating a world where people and animals live together in harmony and love.

29

Illustrator: Neda Kazemifar

ST KATERI TEKAKWITHA

THE 'LILY OF THE MOHAWKS'

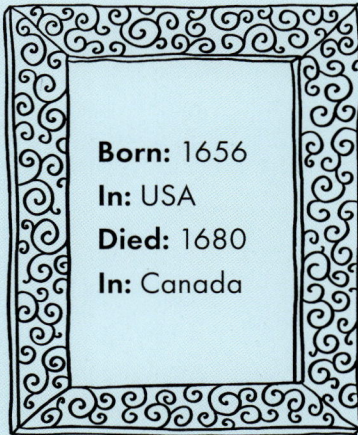

Born: 1656
In: USA
Died: 1680
In: Canada

Have you ever wondered how someone can stay strong and kind even when facing big challenges?

That's exactly what a courageous young girl named Kateri Tekakwitha did.

Born in 1656 in what is now New York, Kateri was a member of the Mohawk tribe of North American Indians. When she was just four years old, the tribe suffered from a devastating outbreak of smallpox, a highly infectious disease that causes a high fever and a rash on the skin. Sadly, many people died, including her family members. Kateri survived the illness, but it left her with visible scars and weakened her health. Her vision was also affected, leading to her being given the name Tekakwitha, which means, "she who bumps into things."

Kateri went to live with her uncle, who eventually became the chief of their tribe. Despite her new home and position, Kateri's life was not easy. From a young age she was expected to help with the hard tasks of collecting wood and water.

At the age of 11, she met Christian missionaries. Missionaries are people who travel around to teach others about their religion and to help communities. The missionaries' teachings and actions made Kateri curious. She had never heard of Jesus, and she felt inspired to find out more. Kateri embraced Christ's teachings and was baptized. It was then that she received the Christian name "Catherine," or Kateri, which was used in her Mohawk language.

When Kateri was 13 years old, a rival tribe attacked her village. It was a frightening time as there was fierce fighting. Leading a group of girls of a similar age, Kateri bravely helped. She looked after the wounded, brought food and water to those who needed it, and buried the dead.

Kateri's commitment to her new faith made life in her village increasingly difficult. She was often threatened and beaten because her community did not accept Christianity. In some cases, she was even pelted with stones.

To avoid the increasing bad feeling towards her, being cruel to her.

During her time at the mission, Kateri dedicated herself to helping others. For instance, she would often try to encourage peaceful relationships between her people and the Christians. She took great care in showing others what it means to forgive someone when they have caused you

Kateri journeyed a remarkable 200 miles to the Christian mission of St Francis Xavier at Sault-Saint-Louis, near Montreal in Canada. There, she became known as the "Lily of the Mohawks" because of her kindness, deep faith, and incredible bravery in remaining true to her beliefs even when people were harm. She taught Native American children about her Christian faith, explaining that Jesus welcomes people of all backgrounds to follow him, showing them love, kindness, and dignity.

Saint Kateri Tekakwitha is the first Native American from the United States to be recognized as a saint by the

Catholic Church. Her life is a powerful example of how people can stay true to their beliefs and help others, even when facing many challenges and difficulties. She teaches us that with bravery and kindness, we can make a meaningful difference in the world.

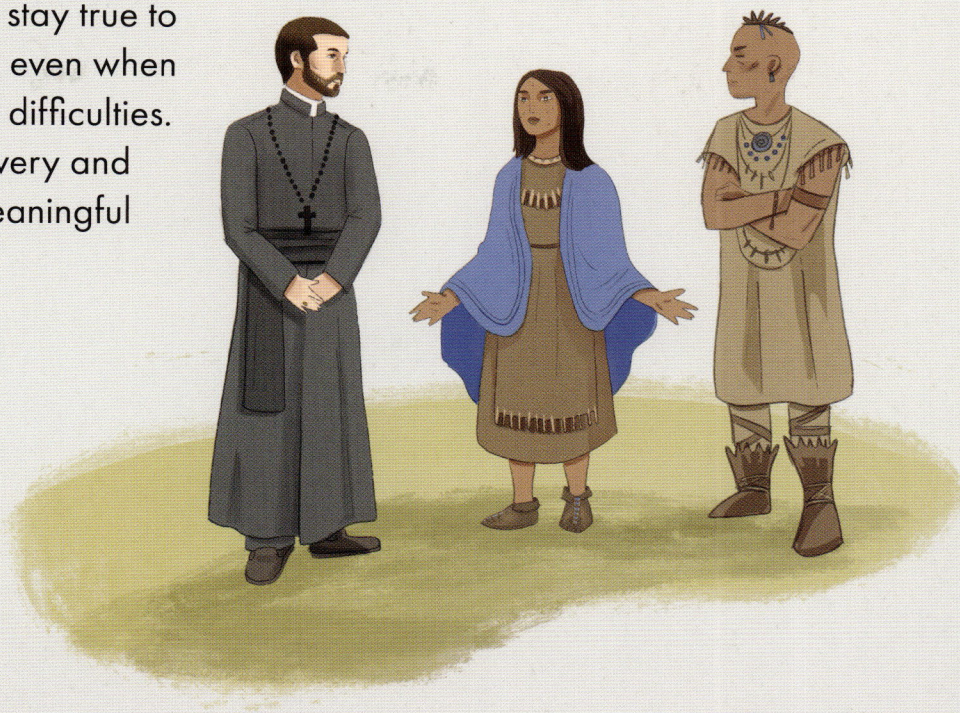

QUESTIONS TO CONSIDER

1. How did Saint Kateri Tekakwitha show bravery and kindness despite the challenges she faced? How can you be brave and kind in your own life?

2. Why do you think Kateri chose to follow her faith and help others so passionately? How can you show kindness and support to people in your community?

3. How can we show understanding and support to people who are different from us, just like Kateri did?

Illustrator: Neda Kazemifar

ST KURIAKOSE ELIAS CHAVARA

A PIONEER OF FREE EDUCATION

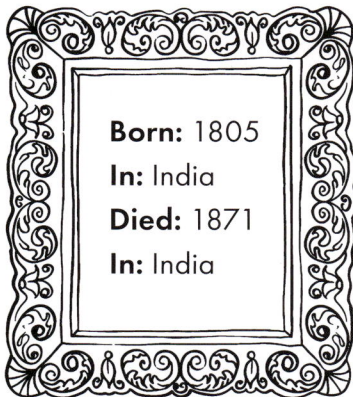

Born: 1805
In: India
Died: 1871
In: India

Can you imagine never having the chance to get an education because you were born into a low caste, or social group? This was the reality for many people born into the lower castes of Indian society in the 19th century. Then, one day, a special man named Kuriakose stepped in and changed things.

Born in 1805, Kuriakose Elias Chavara had a big dream: he wanted every child to have the chance to learn and grow. In his youth, he was deeply devout, regularly attending church and helping those in need. He thought carefully about what he should do when he was grown up.

From an early age he was already busy helping his community. He noticed that many children couldn't go to school because their families struggled to afford the cost. So, he took action and started free schools in the villages of Mannanam and Arpookara. He championed the cause of girls and women in India and led the way in providing education for all children at a time when it was mainly reserved for the wealthy and those who could afford to pay. Kuriakose wanted every child to have the chance to learn, no matter how much money their families had. He made sure that these schools were open to all children and provided a good education.

Kuriakose also knew that children needed to be healthy to do well in school, so he made sure that the schools provided a lunchtime meal. This meal

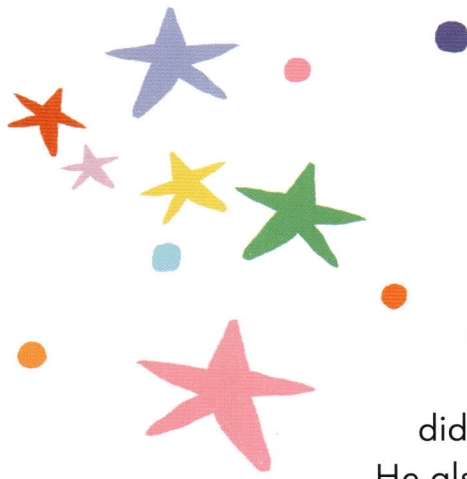

helped the children stay strong and gave them the fuel they needed to learn. But Kuriakose did not stop there. He also worked to improve the lives of people in his community in other ways. For example, he helped build a beautiful home for elderly people who didn't have anyone to take care of them. This home provided them with a safe place to live and made sure they had food and care. Due to his good work, Kuriakose became highly respected in the community where he lived.

As a priest in Koonama, he grew a splendid mango tree. The mangoes tasted so good that Kuriakose wished to share their goodness with everyone. He gave the fruits and seeds to all he encountered, even sending some away to monasteries and convents as a symbol of spreading goodwill.

Kuriakose's faith and strong beliefs guided him in everything he did. He thought it was particularly important to help others and do what was right. Throughout his life Kuriakose continued to work, spreading kindness and offering support wherever he went.

Today, people still remember Kuriakose Elias Chavara for his work and caring heart. In 2014 he was officially made a saint by Pope Francis. Saint

Kuriakose made an enormous difference in many lives by helping children get an education, making sure they were healthy, and taking care of elderly people. His last words before he died show his strong and deep faith: "Why are you sad? All God's people must die someday. My hour has come.

By the grace of God, I prepared myself for it since long . . . Joyfully submit yourselves to the will of God. God is all powerful and His blessings are countless."

QUESTIONS TO CONSIDER

1. What are some of the things Saint Kuriakose Elias Chavara did to help children and elderly people? How did he make sure they had what they needed?

2. Imagine you are Saint Kuriakose Elias Chavara for a day. What would you do to help your community? Write down three things you would prioritize and explain why they are important.

Illustrator: Jen Khatun

PAULINA DLAMINI

A FAITH INFLUENCER

What does it mean to be an influencer? Today the word is often associated with people on social media who talk about and promote products and services, usually to encourage people to buy them. However, throughout history there have been people who have encouraged and persuaded people to work for the good of others. In 1858, a young girl named Nomguqo Dlamini in Northern Zululand, South Africa, embarked on an extraordinary journey that would shape her destiny and help her people.

As the eldest daughter of a Zulu chieftain, Nomguqo's life had a clear path. Because of her position in the Swazi royal family, she was highly regarded by those in her community. The plan was for her to be their future queen. She would marry the Zulu king, Cetshwayo, and together they would lead their people. Her life was filled with a sense of purpose about her future and a deep sense of responsibility towards her tribe. But her journey would take an unexpected turn.

At 13, Nomguqo joined the king's court and became a part of the women's household in preparation for her future. It was there that she met some people who would change her life's path forever. These people were Christian missionaries. At first, she found them amusing. They would share stories from the Bible and entertain the king. But something caught her attention. She noticed how interested the king became whenever the missionaries spoke about the gospel, the stories about Jesus. It was as if there was something special about these stories.

Nomguqo and her family's happy life ended abruptly. The British, who were in charge of South Africa at the time, started a civil war that forced the Zulu king out of the country. The Anglo-Zulu war not only disrupted the royal family's

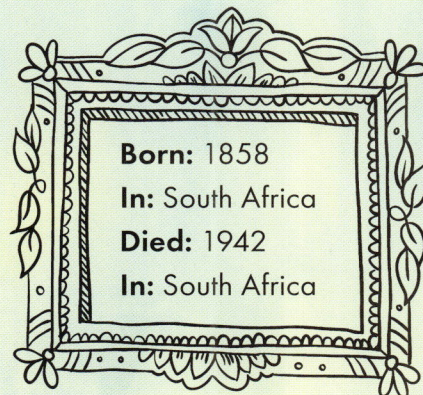

Born: 1858
In: South Africa
Died: 1942
In: South Africa

plans but also led to the loss of many lives and the destruction of homes and livelihoods. Nomguqo and her family were forced to flee and seek shelter with a Dutch farmer. To support her family, Nomguqo and her sister worked as household servants for the farmer, doing their best to make ends meet.

During her time on the Dutch farm, something extraordinary happened. Nomguqo had a vision of a woman glowing in white. This woman urged Nomguqo to explain the Bible to the Zulu people. The vision puzzled her because she couldn't read and wasn't yet a Christian. Confused, Nomguqo shared her vision with the Dutch farmer. He, and others, believed that her visions were from God. The group decided to teach her to read so that she could read the Bible for herself. Nomguqo, who

by that time had changed her name to Paulina, showed a talent for reading and sharing what she learned with others.

For the rest of her life, Paulina devoted herself to serving God and fulfilling his vision for her. She became a key figure in the Zulu community, challenging the unfair treatment that was often carried out by the ruling Dutch authorities. On one occasion, she bravely challenged a Dutch colonizer who was beating his Zulu worker with a stick. Such was her influence that he became a Christian. Her actions included helping to build shelters after the devastation caused by the British, teaching people to read by sharing

the gospel of Jesus Christ, and helping people to stand up for their rights. Her role was significant in shaping the beliefs and customs of the Zulu people.

Paulina's story is remarkable because it reflects how one person can help to spread Christianity within their community, sharing the gospel in ways that are meaningful to them and their culture. It also shows how women like Paulina played a crucial role in supporting their communities and sharing Christian teachings. Their dedication and commitment to the faith, even in places where missionaries had not yet reached, were instrumental in the spread of Christianity in Africa.

QUESTIONS TO CONSIDER

1. Why do you think Paulina found the presence of the Christian missionaries funny at first?

2. Do you think it's important to share your beliefs and values when helping others in the community? Why?

3. What unique talents do you have, and how can you share them to help others?

Illustrator: Amanda Yoshida

BLESSED CEFERINO GIMINEZ MALLA

THE STRONG ONE

Sometimes the power of faith can lead people to do remarkable acts of bravery and kindness. One such person strengthened by faith was Cerefino Giminéz Malla, known as "El Pele," which means "The Strong One." Cerefino was not just strong in body; he was even stronger in character and faith.

Born: 1861
In: Spain
Died: 1936
In: Spain

Cerefino was born in a lively Spanish Romani Gypsy community, where family traditions, dancing, and storytelling were much loved. People often had stereotypes, or widely held beliefs, about Gypsies, thinking they were simply only good for manual work or that they lived in messy conditions. But these stereotypes were unfair, as Cerefino would show throughout his life.

From an early age, Cerefino learned about love, loyalty, and the importance of helping others. His heart was filled with a deep belief in God, and he spent much of his time praying and caring for those around him.

One day, while walking through his village, he stumbled upon a local landowner lying by the road, looking extremely sick. People had passed him by, fearful of catching his illness, but Cerefino's heart told him to stop. "This man needs help," he said to himself. Without a second thought, he

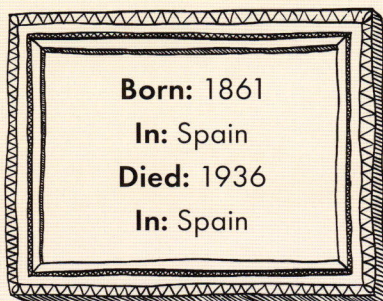

rushed over and lifted the landowner onto his shoulders.

"Don't worry! I will get you home!" he reassured the man, as he carefully carried him back to his caravan. When they arrived, Cerefino helped look after the landowner, nursing him back to health. The landowner's family was so grateful that they gave Cerefino some money. He used the money to start a small business that would support other people who were poor. Cerefino's act of kindness not only saved a life but also changed Cerefino's path, allowing him to help others in his community. Despite the challenges he faced as a Gypsy, Cerefino always stood tall, showing everyone that the stereotypes society had were wrong. He showed that his community could be successful and respectable. He dressed smartly and ran his business with honesty, gaining the trust of the local community. His example inspired many and helped to challenge the negative views about his culture.

Cerefino was known not just for his actions but also for his character. He was good at teaching children and adults about the Christian faith. He was also a respected mediator, helping people settle their disagreements peacefully. He believed that everyone, regardless of their background, deserved to be treated with kindness and respect. Cerefino spent his life bringing together Gypsies and non-Gypsies, showing them that they could learn from each other and live in harmony.

However, Cerefino's life was not without danger. In 1936, during a time of great conflict, he supported priests

44

who were being attacked for their faith. He refused to stop praying, even when it became dangerous. Cerefino was not afraid because he believed in God; his refusal to stop praying and helping others showed his deep faith and courage. Tragically, he was captured and shot dead by a firing squad. Years later, in 1997, Pope John Paul II recognized Cerefino for his extraordinary life in a process known as being "beatified." This means that he would later become a saint in the Catholic Church.

This is significant because Cerefino was the first and only person of Gypsy, Roma, Traveller descent to receive such recognition. His story became a source of hope for many, showing that love and faith can overcome fear and people's opinions.

Cerefino's legacy lives on today. Gypsy, Roma, and Traveller people still share stories of his acts of kindness and bravery. His life reminds us of the power of faith to overcome negative stereotypes and show the world what true strength looks like.

QUESTIONS TO CONSIDER

1. What are some ways that, just like Cerefino, you can show love and compassion to others by bridging gaps and building friendships?

2. Have you ever helped someone in need? How did it make you feel?

3. Why is it important to treat everyone with respect, regardless of their culture and background?

ST JOSEPHINE BAKHITA

A TALE OF TRIUMPH OVER ADVERSITY

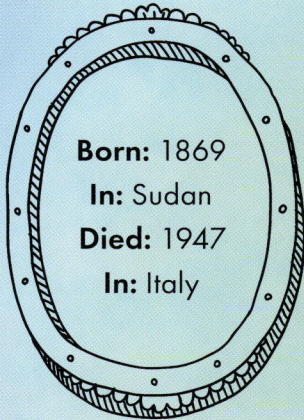

Born: 1869
In: Sudan
Died: 1947
In: Italy

At some point in our lives, we will all go through difficult times. When that happens, we can choose to let our circumstances get the better of us, and give up. Or, like Josephine Bakhita, we can become stronger through these experiences, inspiring others to overcome whatever obstacles they might be facing.

Josephine Bakhita was born in 1869 and grew up in a small village in Sudan. When Josephine was just a young girl, slave traders captured her. They took her away from her family and forced her to work without pay. As an enslaved person, she was treated very cruelly and had no rights. Her life was filled with pain and suffering during these difficult years, when she was "bought" and "sold" many times.

But Josephine never gave up hope. In 1883 she was sold to an official who worked for the Italian government in Sudan. She became the nanny to the official's children. Her life began to change because the family welcomed her, treated her with love and respect, and took her to Italy with them. For the first time, Josephine experienced real kindness, which helped her begin to

heal from all the pain she had suffered.

In Italy, Josephine discovered a new purpose in life. She learned about Christianity and decided to become a nun. Nuns are people who live together in a community and demonstrate their faith by helping others. Josephine took the name "Sister Josephine Bakhita" when she joined the Canossian Sisters. This group of nuns focused on serving people who were poor and sick.

Sister Josephine worked in many places where the Canossian Sisters lived. Josephine visited hospitals and took care of sick people with great love and patience. She made sure they felt cared for by cooking and baking for them, and providing comfort during their illness. Her work went beyond just providing medical help; she also offered emotional support and kindness to everyone she met.

In the Second World War, when bombs fell on the town where she and the sisters lived, she helped and comforted the townspeople and shared their experiences. As the story of her life and reports of her acts of kindness spread, she grew to be loved by many people in Italy.

In addition to her work with sick people, Sister Josephine played a crucial role in teaching and inspiring others. By sharing her own story of overcoming the hardships of slavery, she showed both children and adults that no matter how difficult life can be, there is always hope for a better future. Josephine's experiences encouraged many people to be kinder and more compassionate, showing that even after enduring tough times, faith in God can give us strength to help other people.

One day a student asked Sister Josephine what she would say if she had the chance to meet the people who had enslaved her. Amazingly, rather than

saying that she would punish them for all they had done to her, she told the student she would kneel and kiss their feet. Despite the cruelty she had endured, Sister Josephine found compassion and love for her captors. For this, and for all her work in helping others, Sister Josephine was made a saint in 2000. She is now known as Saint Josephine Bakhita.

QUESTIONS TO CONSIDER

1. Why do you think Sister Josephine chose to help sick people and teach others even though she had faced so many difficulties?

2. Sister Josephine found strength in her faith and her new life. What gives you strength and helps you stay positive when things are tough?

3. What can we learn from Sister Josephine about turning difficult experiences into something good? Can you think of a way you can use something challenging in your life to help others or make a positive difference? Draw or write about a moment when someone's kindness made your heart feel lighter. Share it with a friend or family member, and let the magic of your own kindness shine!

Illustrator: Amanda Yoshida

DR HAROLD MOODY

A BEACON OF UNITY AND COMPASSION

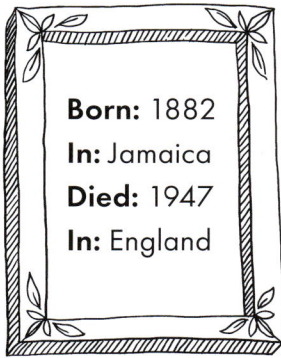

Born: 1882
In: Jamaica
Died: 1947
In: England

Have you ever moved house, or even moved countries? It can be scary enough moving to a new place, but imagine the bravery and determination it takes to be successful in a place that is not welcoming to you because of your background.

In the vibrant city of London in the early 20th century, there was an extraordinary man named Harold Moody. Born in Jamaica in 1882, Harold always dreamed of becoming a doctor. In 1904, he went to London to pursue his dream. Once there, he faced many challenges due to racism, which means that he was treated unfairly because of his race

and where he came from. Despite these difficulties, Harold qualified as a doctor and turned his struggles into opportunities to help others and to fight for fairness.

As a young man, Harold noticed that racial prejudice was everywhere and it was especially hard for Black and Asian people to find good jobs. One of the toughest problems was caused by a law called the Special Restriction Order. This law made it extremely hard for non-British sailors to continue working on commercial ships. Even though during the First World War many of them had fought bravely for Britain, they now lost their jobs.

Inspired by his deep Christian faith, Harold decided to act. He

campaigned against this unfair law and worked hard to change it. Thanks to his efforts, the law was overturned, and many sailors who had been treated unfairly got their jobs back. Harold's determination helped a lot of people who had been struggling to find work.

But Harold did not stop there. He knew that supporting people wasn't just about changing laws; it was also about helping them in their everyday lives. In 1933, he got involved with an institute for Black men, a place set up to help sailors with social and welfare needs. The institute provided support and a sense of community to those who had been facing unfair treatment based on their race and ethnicity, also known as discrimination.

During the Second World War, London was a city filled with challenges. There were bombings and many people needed help. Harold, who was now a respected doctor, played a crucial role in his community. One night in 1944, when a terrible bombing happened in south London, Harold was

one of the first doctors to arrive at the scene. He worked quickly and courageously to help injured people and save lives. His actions showed how dedicated and selfless he was, even in the face of danger.

Harold was also passionate about education. He gave money to students who wanted to learn but did not have much money, providing scholarships to help pay for their education. He believed that everyone deserved a chance to get a good education and build a better future.

Towards the end of his life, Harold went on a speaking tour of North America. He wanted to share his message of fairness and unity with

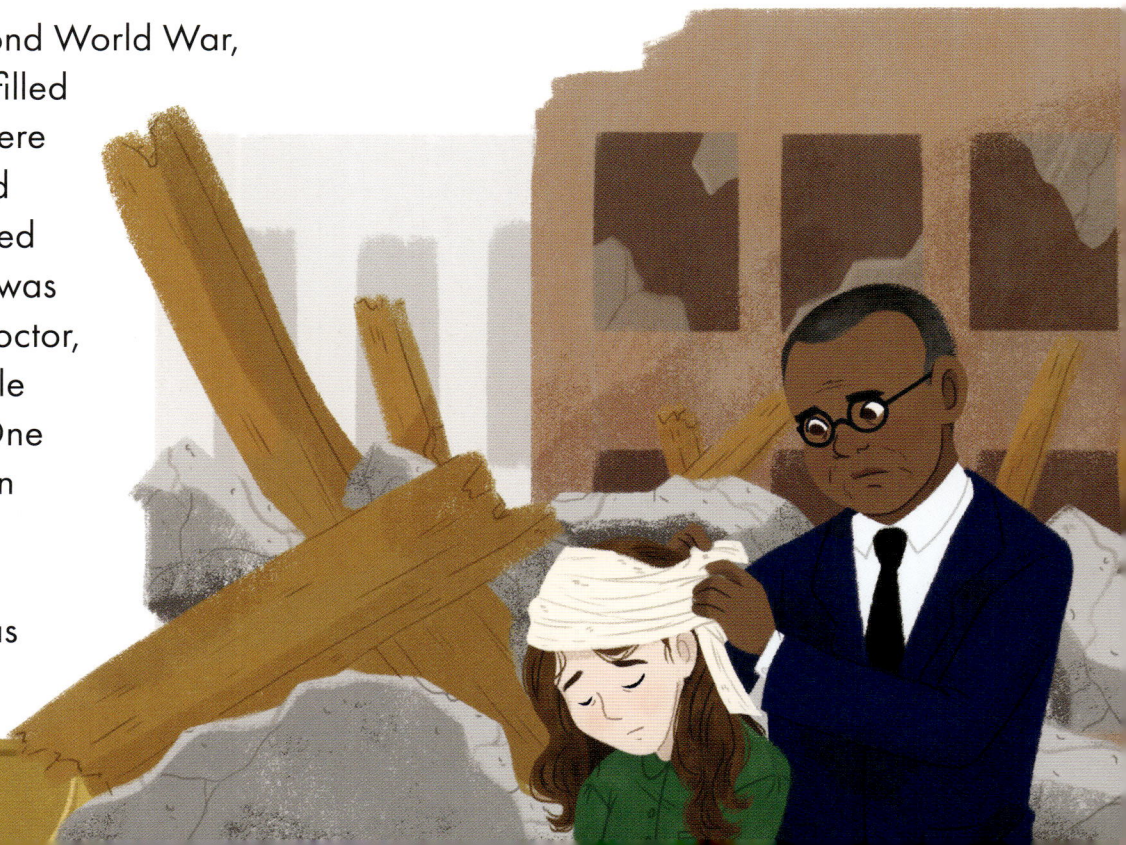

people far beyond London. His travels helped spread his ideas about working together and supporting each other, no matter where you come from.

Harold Moody was a champion for civil rights. Although he didn't live to see it, the work he did laid the foundation for the Race Relations Act in 1965 and helped in the creation of the Race Relations Board in 1966. This was the first law in the UK to make it illegal to mistreat people based on their race or where they came from.

QUESTIONS TO CONSIDER

1. Why do you think Dr Harold Moody chose to fight against unfair laws and help his community, even when it was hard?

2. How can you use your own talents and abilities to help others and make a positive impact in your community, just like Harold did?

3. Dr Moody helped many people during tough times. Can you think of a way you can support someone who might need help or encouragement right now?

Illustrator: Ashley Evans

TOYOHIKO KAGAWA

A PEACEMAKER AND COMMUNITY BUILDER

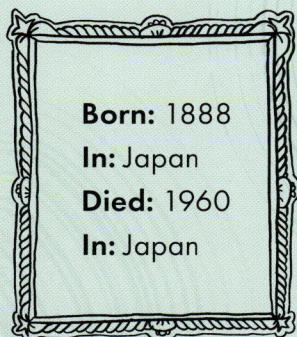

Born: 1888
In: Japan
Died: 1960
In: Japan

Throughout history, especially in times of uncertainty and change such as war, there have been kind people who fought for the rights of others. They stand out because of their selfless dedication to helping others.

Toyohiko Kagawa was like this. He was an important figure in the history of Japan, known for his Christian values and commitment to social change. He believed strongly that, as a Christian, he had a duty not only to read and preach about God's Word but also to live out the gospel in his actions.

In particular, he felt that he needed to help the poorest people in society. He did not agree that they should be forced to live in slums and wanted them to be treated more fairly. At that time, people with Toyohiko's level of education could get well-paid jobs, but that was not for him. Despite criticism for his lack of official training as a Christian pastor, Toyohiko's actions and writings showed a deep understanding of faith and a strong commitment to social justice.

In 1909, Toyohiko moved into a Kobe slum, where he lived with those who were poor, to show Christian love and support. Because of his efforts, the people in the community had enough food to eat. They also started to feel

proud of what they had and learned to take care of their resources. This helped make their community a better place to live.

Toyohiko's goal was to make communities more independent. In one project, members were encouraged to grow different types of crops, including walnuts. Toyohiko helped them to plant walnut trees not only to provide food for the people, but also to help feed their pigs and other animals.

The project aimed to create a system where both people and animals could benefit, through combining farming the land with caring for the animals. The main goal of this project was to help the community to support itself. This was very important because many people did not have much money. But when they put their resources together, they could provide for everyone. By teaching people how to farm in a sustainable way and encouraging them to be independent, Toyohiko wanted to help others solve the problem of not having enough food and to promote a healthier lifestyle.

Toyohiko also worked hard to help improve lives by creating unions to protect the rights of workers, supporting voting rights for all.

By the mid-1920s, his efforts to help the poorest people made him a national figure in Japan. His influence reached a global scale. He went overseas to countries like the United States, where he met with important people such as Mahatma Gandhi (an Indian social activist) and Albert Einstein (a German scientist).

Despite his growing fame, Toyohiko faced a lot of opposition from those who had a strong devotion to their country.

Nationalism was on the rise in Japan, which means that people felt that their country was superior to other nations. People like Toyohiko, who did not share this belief, were often treated badly.

Toyohiko's strong beliefs in peace and non-violence meant he was known as a pacifist. This made him unpopular, and, when he also apologized for Japan's occupation of China, he was arrested. Nevertheless, he remained committed to his principles of peace and that people should live together in harmony. As the Second World War approached, Toyohiko tried to promote peace during his visits to America. Then war broke out, and he returned to Japan.

After the war, Toyohiko played an important role in reconstruction, helping in the process of rebuilding Japan. He turned down offers of senior political roles to serve as an advisor to the new Japanese government. His contributions to workers movements, cooperative efforts, and the books he wrote reflected his vision of creating a new society founded on love and respect for every person, inspired by his Christian faith.

QUESTIONS TO CONSIDER

1. How did Toyohiko Kagawa's Christian faith inspire him to help those in need and stand up for social justice?

2. What challenges did Kagawa face while promoting peace and opposing nationalism in Japan?

3. Do you have a local foodbank in your community that helps people who need extra support? If your family is able to, perhaps you could buy some extra food the next time you go shopping and donate it to the foodbank.

Illustrator: Anastasia Magloire Williams

TSAI 'CHRISTIANA' SU JUAN

THE QUEEN OF THE DARK CHAMBER

Born: 1890
In: China
Died: 1984
In: USA

Imagine being confined to bed for 22 years for poor health. Now imagine being so full of joy that people would come to see you not to cheer you up, but for you to encourage them! This is what happened to Tsai Su Juan, who was also known as Christiana. But what made Su Juan so joyful despite her illness? The clue is in her story of faith.

Su Juan was born in 1890, one of 24 children. She grew up in a comfortable home as the daughter of a vice governor of Kiangsu, a province in China. She was known as the seventh sister, "Miss Seven" or "Too Many." The name was not meant to be cruel but to reflect her position in her large, wealthy family. However, she often felt sorrowful, as many of her family members were addicted to the drug opium.

Although she considered becoming a Buddhist nun and living a life of self-denial, she decided to help her family. Her interest in the English language led

her to attend a school run by missionaries. There, she not only learned English but also learned about Jesus Christ and became a Christian.

As Su Juan's faith grew stronger, she wanted to share the message of God's hope with her family. Despite facing opposition from them due to her conversion to Christianity, Su Juan found inner peace and joy through her newfound faith. She read the Bible and prayed a lot, deepening her relationship with Christ. After graduation, Su Juan turned down important job offers. Instead, she returned home to share the gospel with her family and community. In addition to sharing the story of her faith with family and friends, she would preach about Jesus by her local river. Her perseverance paid off! Eventually, 55 members of her family became Christians including her mother.

In 1931, Su Juan became ill with severe malaria, a disease carried by mosquitos, and developed other conditions that left her in bed for lengthy periods of time. She became sensitive to light and noise and had to stay in a darkened room. Despite her challenges, Su Juan continued to minister to others, offering encouragement during their visits and by writing letters. She often remarked that her bed was not a prison but a training school, with the Holy Spirit as her mentor and her visitors as her homework.

The things she wrote reached a wide audience and inspired thousands to attend events where, when she was well enough, she passionately preached the Word of God. Her words were so powerful that she became known as the "Queen of the Dark Chamber" for her unwavering faith and dedication to serving Christ. During the Second World War, Su Juan faced

even more difficulties. The Japanese occupied China, imprisoning missionaries, including the principal of her school, Miss Leaman. Despite the constant threat of being put in prison and having little food and water, she continued to spread the message of Christ alongside Miss Leaman when she was released.

After the war, Su Juan moved to Pennsylvania in America, where she wrote her autobiography, *Queen of the Dark Chamber*. Her passion to share God's Word also prompted her to help develop the first phonetic Bible for Chinese people who could not read. This means that people could sound out the words rather than have to memorize the Chinese characters. When she was too ill to distribute her work to people

herself, she relied on a cat to help her. From her "dark chamber," she would tie small handouts that told the story of the gospel onto the cat's collar, and the cat would carry them to the people.

Even though she faced many challenges, in the first few pages of her book there is a quote that captures Su Juan's attitude: "A sage sees opportunities in difficulties, but a fool finds problems in opportunities." This means that to be wise you need to see what good can come out of tricky situations.

QUESTIONS TO CONSIDER

1. How did Tsai Su Juan's faith and dedication to Christ inspire others to believe?

2. What opportunities do you think can come from some of the difficulties around friendships in your community today?

3. Can you think of a time when someone cheered you up or encouraged you? What did they say or do? What hope or good news can you share with someone today, write a card or draw a picture to let them know.

Illustrator: Ashley Evans

INI KOPURIA

A PIONEER BRIDGING FAITH AND CULTURE

If God spoke to you, telling you to change your life, would you listen? Or would you dig your heels in and pretend you didn't hear anything? Ini Kopuria chose to listen, and God's call took him on a very different path than what he expected.

Ini lived in Guadalcanal, one of the main Solomon Islands. As a young boy he was thoughtful and reflective. He also loved nature and dreamed of great adventures. When he thought about what he might do as a grown-up, the possibilities were endless. Perhaps he would sail across the ocean, be a farmer, or help others? His teachers saw his potential to become a teacher, but Ini had different ideas.

He joined the Solomon Islands Police Force. He excelled at his job, and worked tirelessly in his local community to keep the peace. But a motorcycle accident would change his life forever.

The accident left him in bed with serious injuries. Although it was painful and there were difficult times, Ini started to think about what God wanted him to do with the rest of his life. Then, as Ini started to recover, he experienced a powerful vision of Christ. In this vision, Christ told him that he was not doing the work he was meant to do.

The vision inspired him to leave behind his career in the police force and dedicate himself to declaring the kingdom of God to whoever would listen. Seeking guidance, Ini approached his bishop, John Steward, who could see he had a strong, deep belief. Bishop Steward sent him to study theology to find out more about God and what it means to live out faith.

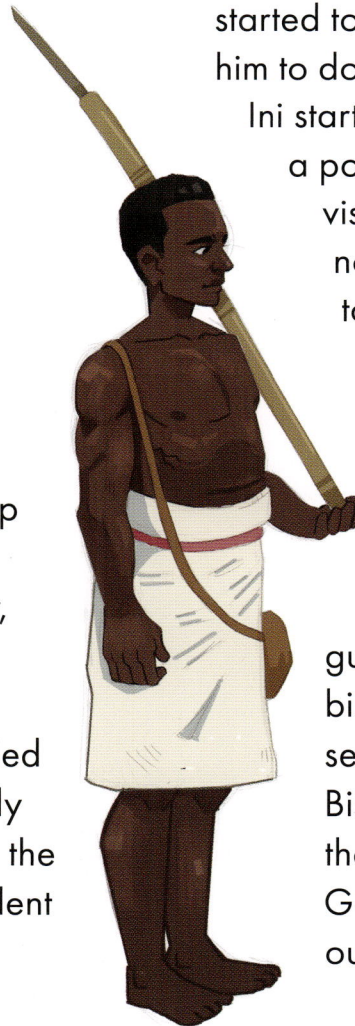

> **Born:** around 1900
> **In:** Solomon Islands
> **Died:** 1945
> **In:** Solomon Islands

On this religious training course, Ini learned about the teachings of Saint Francis of Assisi and European monasteries. Saint Francis was known for his care of people who were poor and his love of nature. Saint Francis also founded an order, or group of people who decide they will live and pray together in a special community. Saint Francis' order, known as Franciscans, demonstrated love for nature, animals, and their fellow human beings.

Inspired by these teachings, Ini thought he, too, could gather a group together who wanted to live like that, but in a way familiar to the Solomon islanders. After much thought, Ini started the Melanesian Brotherhood, a group of missionary brothers committed to reaching areas where other missionaries could not. The Brothers lived in small community households. They took vows of poverty, obedience, and celibacy, which means never marrying.

The Brotherhood's mission work involved living in local communities, preaching the message of Christ, providing practical help, and supporting communities with their crops and animals.

Members of the Brotherhood shared what little they had. Ini farmed his land to provide food for the Brotherhood, making sure they had the food and materials needed for their mission work.

Despite Ini's early death at the age of 43, his legacy lived on through the continued work of the Brotherhood. In 1979, the Sisters of Melanesia were

established to serve the women of the islands, following the example set by the Melanesian Brotherhood.

Ini's life reflected the harmonious blend of faith and culture, presenting Christianity in a way that connected with his people. His commitment to respecting cultural identities while sharing the message of Christ has made an impact on many people. The Melanesian Brotherhood still continue Ini's visionary spirit, inspiring many generations after him to embrace their cultural heritage as they carry out their mission work.

Today, the Brother and Sisterhood are as dedicated to serving others with love and understanding as Ini was. His story serves as a reminder of the importance of bridging the gap between faith and culture, conveying messages in a way that connects to transform lives through practical work.

QUESTIONS TO CONSIDER

1. How did Ini Kopuria's vision of Christ inspire him to change his career and dedicate his life to serving others?

2. Why do you think it is important to share the message of Christ in a way that speaks to different cultures?

3. How can we follow Ini's example of blending faith and culture to positively impact our communities?

Illustrator: Richy Sanchez Ayala

FLORENCE LI TIM-OI

THE FIRST FEMALE ANGLICAN PRIEST

Discrimination means not allowing someone the same opportunities as another person because of such things as their gender, age, or background. Throughout the history of the Protestant Church, women have faced some discrimination. In the Church of England, women were not officially allowed to be priests until 1994, when Angela Berners-Wilson became the first woman to be ordained, or made a priest. However, Angela was not the first in the world. Many years before, in 1944, Florence Li Tim-Oi became the first female Anglican priest, ever.

What is surprising is that Florence Li Tim-Oi did not set out on this path. She was born in the little fishing village of Aberdeen, part of Hong Kong, in 1907. Her father, a doctor, had changed his career to become the headteacher of the local government-run school. At the time, some of the old ideas meant people were valued differently,

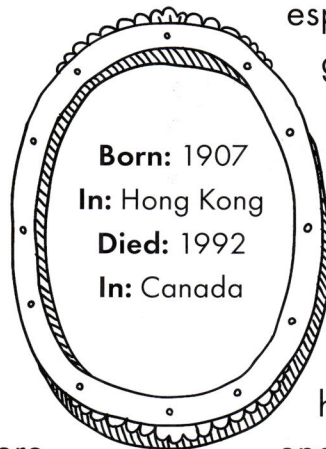

Born: 1907
In: Hong Kong
Died: 1992
In: Canada

especially girls. However, Mr Li gave his daughter the name "Tim-Oi," which means "another much-beloved girl." His greatest wish was for her to be happy and well-loved despite living in a culture that often valued sons over daughters. Although her parents were Christian, they encouraged their children to respect their cultural traditions while embracing modern ways. He encouraged her to read and learn.

Growing up, Li Tim-Oi became an

active member of her local Anglican church, helping whenever needed. She embraced the Christian faith and added "Florence" to her name after the famous nurse Florence Nightingale, known for her dedication to helping others.

At a time when only men were permitted to train as priests, Florence Li Tim-Oi dared to dream of a different path. One day, she heard an English woman offer to serve in the church and wondered if a Chinese woman could do the same. Kneeling in prayer, Florence questioned if she was the right person to help in this way.

After much prayer, Florence Li Tim-Oi felt a deep belief that God wanted her to be a deacon, a person who serves others in the church and community. Despite the challenges and social expectations, she enrolled in a seminary, a college that would prepare her for religious leadership and service. She graduated in 1938. As war loomed over China and Japanese armies advanced, Florence found herself in Macau, a Portuguese colony within China where many people had fled for safety. In Macau she was able to help people as a deacon, but because of the war, there were no male priests. People could not fully participate in church life; there were some parts of the service only a male priest could lead. Florence Li Tim-Oi went to see her bishop, the senior leader in the area, to ask if she could help. Much to her surprise, the bishop said yes.

So, on 25 January 1944, she made history by becoming the first woman to be officially made a priest in the Anglican Church. Following her ordination, Florence Li Tim-Oi served as the leading minister at St Barnabas Church, where she established schools and a maternity home for pregnant women and new mothers in need.

During her time in Macau, Florence Li Tim-Oi dedicated herself to caring for sick people, educating children, assisting the less fortunate, and supporting the elderly. However, political changes forced her to leave. When the communist regime took control, they closed the country's borders from 1958 to 1974 and brought in strict laws. During that time, Florence Li Tim-Oi was forced to work on a farm and in a government factory. Because of her Christian faith, she faced persecution, which means being mistreated for her beliefs and restricted in what she could do. But Li Tim-Oi's strong faith helped her to persevere despite these challenges. She even gave up her priest's license to protect those who had ordained her during a dangerous time in China. Eventually, Li Tim-Oi left China to live in Canada.

In 1984, after over 30 years, Li Tim-Oi had the opportunity to be a priest again in Toronto, Canada, where her ministry continued to inspire others. Florence Li Tim-Oi paved the way for other women to pursue the priesthood.

QUESTIONS TO CONSIDER

1. How did Florence Li Tim-Oi's faith inspire her to become the first female priest in the worldwide Anglican Church?

2. Why is Florence's determination to serve in a role traditionally reserved for men important for us today?

3. What can we learn from Florence's story about resilience, faith, and helping others in need?

Illustrator: Samya Zitouni

OSEOLA McCARTY

A SELFLESS GIFT OF GENEROSITY

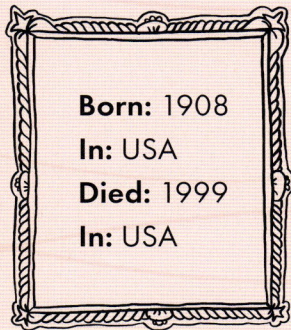

Born: 1908
In: USA
Died: 1999
In: USA

Did you know that a gift given with a good heart can make an enormous difference in the lives of many? The story of Oseola McCarty shows how a selfless act of generosity can open up new and exciting opportunities for others.

Oseola McCarthy was born in Mississippi, USA in 1908. From age 11, Oseola worked hard to help her family with their laundry and ironing business. Every penny she earned was placed carefully in her pink doll's pram; she wanted to go to college in her home state of Mississippi one day, to study and become a nurse. It was a huge dream. Poor people like Oseola rarely went to college, because tuition fees were very expensive.

Sadly, Oseola's dream of becoming a nurse was put on hold when she had to leave school, aged 12, to care for her sick aunt. Looking after people was something Oseola did naturally. Inspired by her Christian faith, she believed that people got a sense of purpose from work. It did not matter what that work was, but the idea was to do your best. Oseola knew that doing small things over time can make a huge difference. She also knew that she couldn't help everyone. She said, "I can't do everything. But I can do something to help somebody. And what I can do, I will do."

Despite facing challenges and setbacks, Oseola continued working, washing and ironing other people's laundry tirelessly for 75 years, until arthritis made it too difficult for her to continue. She was a quiet lady who regularly went to church and believed in Jesus' message of thinking about others.

Oseola did not go on any holidays, or even buy new clothes and shoes. Instead, she wore hand-me-down clothes, and when her shoes became worn, she simply mended them herself or cut out the toes of second-hand shoes that were too small. Then one day, at the age of 87, Oseola made a huge, life-changing decision that touched the hearts of many people.

After years of saving, she decided to give away all her money. By that time, she had saved quite a bit. Can you imagine giving away all your life savings to help others? In 1995, Oseola donated $150,000 to the University of Southern Mississippi. This generous gift created the Oseola McCarty Scholarship Endowment, which has since helped over 160 students who could not afford to get a university degree to follow their college dreams. Oseola's act of kindness gave these students the opportunity to receive an education and strive for their goals.

Her generosity went on to inspire others to give to the college fund. Donations poured in, and the fund grew. In the months that followed, more than 600 people added another $330,000. This incredible sum of money is still making a difference to the lives of many young people today. In one newspaper interview, Oseola said, "You have to accept God the best you know how… the more you serve God, the more able

you are to serve God."

Oseola's story serves as a reminder of the power of hard work, determination, and the desire to help others. Despite facing hardships and not having the opportunity to pursue a formal education herself, Oseola found a way to make a lasting difference through her kindness and generosity. Although she wasn't rich or powerful, her selfless gift highlights how one person's act of kindness can positively impact the lives of many, creating a ripple effect of goodness and hope. We can all make a difference in the lives of others. Whether it's through sharing our time, talents, or resources, we can spread kindness and bring about positive change.

QUESTIONS TO CONSIDER

1. How might Oseola McCarty's scholarship fund help students who receive her gift?

2. What can we learn from Oseola's story about the importance of helping others and making a difference in the world?

3. How can you follow Oseola's example of kindness and selflessness? What small acts of generosity can you show others?

Illustrator: Anastasia Magloire Williams

ST ALPHONSA

A LIFE OF SACRIFICE FOR OTHERS

Born: 1910
In: India
Died: 1946
In: India

Sometimes, when we aren't feeling well, it is easy to lose faith and blame God for our suffering. Saint Alphonsa did the complete opposite: she thanked God for her suffering and saw her life as a sacrifice that made her feel closer to Jesus. Not only that, she saw her suffering as a way of understanding the hurt and pain of others, showing true compassion.

Annakutty, who would later be known as Saint Alphonsa, grew up in a peaceful village in India. A kind-hearted and compassionate person, she cared deeply for those around her. After the death of her mother, Annakutty often spent time with her grandmother, listening to stories and Christian songs. From a young age, she learned the values of community and empathy, and the importance of helping others in need.

As Annakutty grew older, she faced many challenges, including long periods of illness and hardship. Once she fell into a pit of burning wheat and her feet were severely burned. She spent several weeks in bed and was left with painful scars and injuries that troubled her for the rest of her life. Later, she suffered from typhoid fever, which made her very weak. She also had a leg deformity caused by an untreated

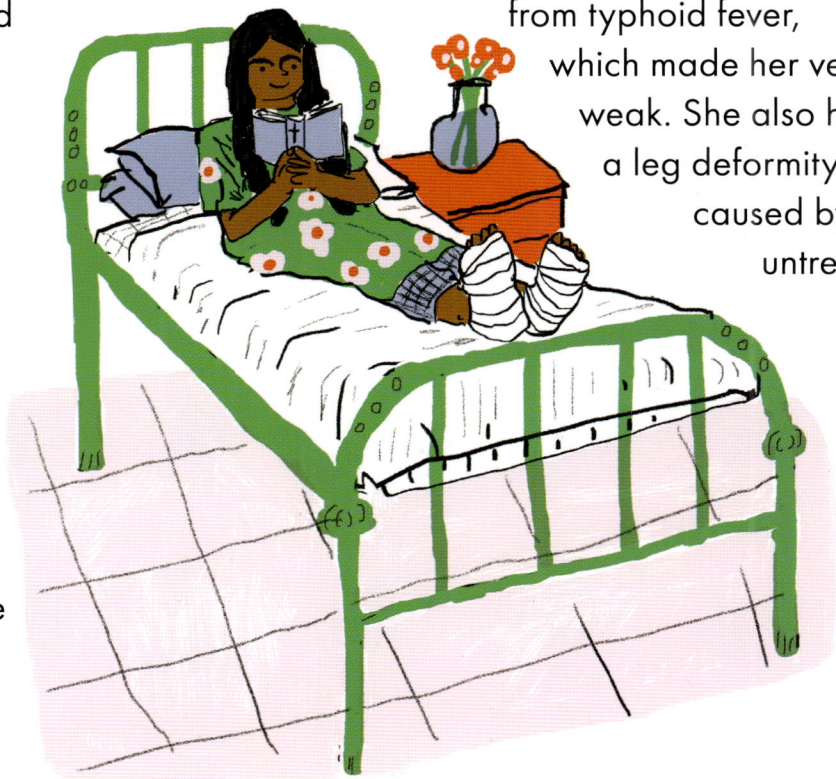

fracture, and she suffered from shaking fits called convulsions and other painful conditions.

Even though she was often in pain and extremely sick, Annakutty always put the needs of others before her own. She saw her pain as a way of helping her to understand and share the pain of others, as if she were in their shoes. This great ability to relate to others and show compassion for those who were suffering led her to dedicate her life to serving people. She became a nun and took the name Alphonsa. She devoted herself to a life of prayer and helping those in need, always thinking about how she could help others feel better.

Alphonsa was also dedicated to teaching and inspiring children. She shared stories about kindness, faith, and compassion, helping children understand the importance of being caring and loving. Her gentle and encouraging words helped many young people grow up with strong values and a sense of empathy for others.

Throughout her life, Alphonsa demonstrated incredible self-sacrifice. She endured physical pain and illness with humility, often thinking of other people first and praying for them rather than herself. Her faith and commitment to helping others inspired those around her to believe and brought hope to many who were in despair.

In recognition of her kindness and dedication, Alphonsa was

76

declared a saint by the Catholic Church. She was the first woman of Indian background to become a saint. Her story continues to inspire people around the world to live with compassion and help those in need. Saint Alphonsa shows us that even when we face our own struggles, we can find comfort and strength in our faith and put others' needs before our own.

QUESTIONS TO CONSIDER

1. Why do you think Saint Alphonsa chose to help others even when she was sick and in pain?

2. How do you think Saint Alphonsa's actions, like caring for people who were sick and teaching children, helped those around her? What is one way you can show kindness and help someone in your own life?

3. Think of a time that you faced a challenge or felt sad, and someone in your life showed you kindness and compassion, like Saint Alphonsa did for others. Draw a picture or write a letter to that person, thanking them for their support and sharing how their actions made you feel.

Illustrator: Jen Khatun

PAULI MURRAY

A CIVIL RIGHTS ACTIVIST

Have you ever been stopped from doing something just for being you? What did you do? At a time when not everyone was treated equally, Pauli Murray showed great courage by standing up for justice and speaking out against racial inequality in America. Many African Americans did not have the same opportunities as others and faced harsh discrimination in housing, jobs, and education.

Pauli grew up in Maryland in the USA. She had a difficult childhood, losing both parents at a young age. After teaching herself to read at five, she found comfort in books. Reading opened her imagination to what was possible, and she dreamed of an America in which all people were treated equally and with respect. Even as a teenager she had a strong sense of right and wrong, refusing to ride on buses or attend cinemas where Black people were forced to sit separately

Born: 1910
In: USA
Died: 1985
In: USA

from White people. She did well at school and later became a teacher in New York, where she used her talent for writing to support various causes. She faced some difficult times, but Pauli kept writing about what she believed in. Her articles, published in magazines, reflected her passion for fair treatment and equality for all. She also wrote poetry, putting into words the feelings, disappointments and hopes Black people had. Through her work, she caught the attention of Eleanor Roosevelt, herself a powerful supporter of human rights and the wife of the President of the United States. The First Lady became a friend and supporter in Pauli's fight for justice.

Pauli decided that she could make more of an impact if she studied law, so she applied to law school. At a time when African Americans and women could only attend certain colleges, she applied to any that would offer her a

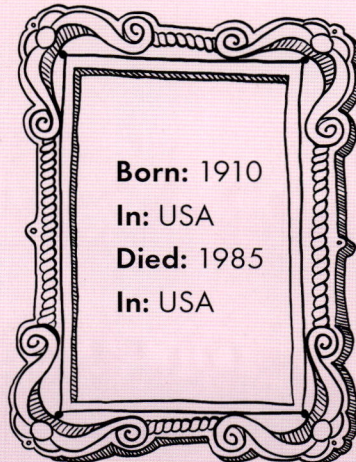

good education. Pauli was denied admission to the all-White University of North Carolina. But she didn't give up. Instead, she enrolled in Howard University in Washington, DC, where she graduated top of her class. In one lesson, a professor declared he didn't know why women wanted to study law, because they would be no good at it. With fierce determination, Pauli set out to not only prove him wrong, but show that she could be the best.

At university she helped to create the Congress of Racial Equality. Through this organization, she promoted peaceful protests to bring attention to the fight for justice and equality through her law work. But it did not stop there. The group participated in "sit ins," in which protestors sat down and refused to move, to draw attention to their cause. Pauli also wrote passionately to different authorities to put forward the case for equal treatment. Despite facing gender and racial discrimination herself, and being rejected from Harvard University, Pauli continued her legal studies at the University of California, Berkeley. She

put her knowledge to good use as one of the few African-American female lawyers at the time.

Pauli recognized that her faith inspired her to help others, acting as a source of healing. She felt that her work should cut across all divisions to bring hope in the face of obstacles and challenges. In 1977 she became the first Black woman in the United States to become a priest. She promoted equality and inclusion and faced discrimination with courage, honesty, insight, and integrity. Pauli Murray's remarkable journey from teacher to lawyer, and poet to priest, is genuinely inspiring, showing her perseverance and dedication to fighting for justice and equality.

Although the United States now has laws that say people must not be discriminated against due to their race or gender, there is still a need to challenge unfairness in society. Pauli's impact lives on through her pioneering work in the American civil rights movement, as well as in her writing. Her courageous spirit shows the power of resilience and determination in the face of hardship.

Standing up for justice and equality often requires bravery, but it can lead to positive change for ourselves and those around us.

QUESTIONS TO CONSIDER

1. Have you ever needed to stand up for what is right, even if it was difficult? If you did, what impact did it have on you and others?

2. Why is it important to treat everyone equally and challenge discrimination, like Pauli Murray did?

3. How can we show resilience and determination in our own lives when faced with obstacles?

Illustrator: Ana Latese

ROSA PARKS

A WOMAN WHO REFUSED TO MOVE

Have you ever wondered what it takes to act and speak out for what is right, even when it's difficult and could mean trouble? For one woman, Rosa Parks, a single act of rebellion against unfair laws led to changes that rippled across the United States.

Rosa was born in Montgomery, Alabama. Rosa was known for her strong sense of right and wrong, inspired by her Christian beliefs. She believed that everyone should be treated with kindness and respect, no matter their racial background.

Born: 1913
In: USA
Died: 2005
In: USA

During Rosa's time, there were many unfair rules that treated African Americans differently in a system called segregation: the practice of keeping people of different races separate, often in an unequal way. For example, on buses, there were separate sections for White people and Black people. White people could sit at the front of the bus, while Black people had to sit at the back. Shops and restaurants had "Whites Only" sections that separated people. As a young girl, Rosa saw these signs and felt how unfair they were. She would often think, "Will this ever change?"

One December evening in 1955, Rosa Parks got on a bus and took a seat in the "Black" section. When the bus became full, the driver told Rosa

WHITES ONLY

determination cover my body like a quilt on a winter night." She was arrested for her refusal to move but was released on bail.

Her brave action resulted in a tremendous change. Inspired by her courage, the people in her community decided to do something about these unfair rules. This led to a major protest known as the Montgomery Bus Boycott.

During the boycott, many people in Montgomery chose not to ride the buses. Instead, they walked or found other ways to get around. This showed how strong and united they were in their fight against segregation. In the end, the boycott lasted for 381 days. During this time, the bus company lost a lot of money due to buses not being used. Eventually, the city changed the law requiring segregation on public buses. The people of Montgomery proved that they could fight for their rights and make a difference.

In recognition of her courageous actions, which brought attention to unjust laws, Rosa Parks received numerous awards, including the Presidential Medal of Freedom in 1996 and the Congressional Gold Medal in 1999. These awards celebrated her role in

and some other Black passengers to give up their seats so White people could sit there instead. Rosa was tired of always having to give in to rules that privileged one race over another. She could have just moved to avoid trouble, but she decided to do what she believed was right.

Rosa calmly refused to move. She felt that this rule was wrong and that everyone should have equal rights, including where they could sit on the bus. Years later, she remembered, "When that White driver stepped back toward us, when he waved his hand and ordered us up and out of our seats, I felt a advancing civil rights and inspiring others. A museum dedicated to her life and legacy, the Rosa Parks Museum, was established at Troy University in Montgomery. It serves as a place where people can learn about her contributions to the civil rights movement, which aimed to eliminate racial discrimination and to recognize the rights of every individual.

Rosa Parks' dedication to justice continues to inspire people to stand up for their rights and work towards a world where everyone has the same opportunities to achieve their best. Rosa Parks' story is a great example of how one person's bravery can make a big difference.

QUESTIONS TO CONSIDER

1. Why do you think Rosa Parks chose to stay in her seat on the bus, even though it was against the rules at that time?

2. How did Rosa Parks' actions help bring about change in her community?

3. What is one thing you can do in your own life to stand up for fairness and help others who might be treated unfairly?

Illustrator: Amanda Quartey

ARCHBISHOP OSCAR ROMERO

A VOICE FOR JUSTICE

Sometimes standing up for your beliefs can be difficult, even dangerous. For Oscar Romero, his faith demanded that he not only pray for change, but also actively try to help the most needy and vulnerable people. And in this mission, he would make the ultimate sacrifice.

From a young age, Oscar noticed how important it was for people to support each other. His childhood experiences of being poor made him believe in the power of community; it was normal for him to see people sharing food and working together to overcome problems.

In El Salvador, it was not unusual for poor children to have to go to work. At age 14, Oscar was working by candlelight in damp conditions under the ground, chipping at rocks for gold. Such an experience shaped his views because he knew what it was to be cold and hungry. As he grew up, he felt a strong desire to help those who were being mistreated, and to fight for fair treatment and justice for everyone.

Oscar became a priest, then an archbishop. He used this position to speak out against the many problems affecting his country. One of his notable actions was his public criticism of the government's brutal treatment of its citizens. For instance, he used his Sunday morning sermons and radio broadcasts to speak out against

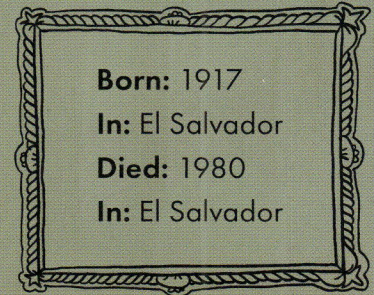

Born: 1917
In: El Salvador
Died: 1980
In: El Salvador

the military's violence, urging soldiers to disobey orders that resulted in harming innocent people. This was a brave move because criticizing the government could mean you went to prison, or even worse, were killed.

Another important action Archbishop Romero took was in response to the murder of his friend, Father Rutilio Grande. Father Grande had been killed because he openly criticized the government's unfair treatment of people who were poor. Oscar was deeply affected by this tragedy. He spoke out against his friend's murder, and highlighted the need for justice and protection for the vulnerable. He dedicated many of his speeches and sermons to calling for an end to violence and injustice, which put him at great personal risk.

Oscar also took special care to help children who were suffering due to poverty, violence, and mistreatment. He supported efforts to improve education for poor children. He worked with local schools to ensure that children from poor backgrounds were able to go to school and get educational resources. He understood that education was a key to breaking

the cycle of poverty and violence.

In a country where many children were suffering from malnutrition and disease, Oscar spoke up for proper medical care and nutritional support. He argued that healthcare should be accessible to all families in need. Oscar made visits to schools and health clinics to see the conditions firsthand and to offer encouragement. He believed that by supporting children, he could help build a better future for El Salvador.

Despite the constant threats and bullying from government authorities, extremist groups, and terrorist gangs, Oscar Romero remained steadfast in his commitment to justice. He knew the risks but believed his mission was more

important. His courage and dedication earned him respect and admiration from many people, though it also made him a target for those who opposed his message.

In 1980, while he was celebrating mass in a hospital chapel, Oscar's life was tragically cut short. He was shot and killed by gunmen who were against his messages of peace, love, and justice. This act of violence shocked many and highlighted the dangers faced by those who stand up for what is right. Despite his early death, Oscar's legacy lives on. His courage and commitment to justice have inspired countless people to continue his work for a fairer and more compassionate world.

Archbishop Oscar Romero's story is a powerful example of what true strength and compassion look like.

QUESTIONS TO CONSIDER

1. Why do you think Oscar Romero chose to speak out against injustice even though it was dangerous? What made him keep going despite the risks?

2. How can you show courage and kindness in your own life to help others who may be treated unfairly?

3. What are some ways you can stand up for what is right in your community?

ARCHBISHOP DESMOND TUTU
A CHAMPION OF HOPE

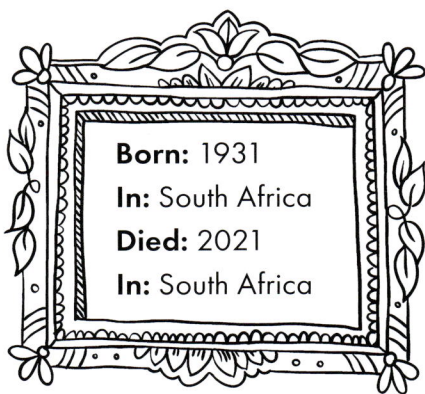

Born: 1931
In: South Africa
Died: 2021
In: South Africa

Should we forgive those who cause great harm to us or others? Jesus preached a message of forgiving our enemies, but putting these teachings into practice can be very difficult. Yet this is exactly what Desmond Tutu did. Not only did he work to make changes to a very unfair and harmful system, but he also understood the power of forgiveness.

Born in 1931, Desmond witnessed many unfair things happening to people of different races in his home country of South Africa. This motivated him to want to work to make things better. Apartheid (or "apart-hood") was a system in South Africa that enforced racial segregation and discrimination, where the government privileged White people over other racial and ethnic groups. Black people couldn't live in the same areas, use the same facilities, or have the same rights as White people.

From an early age, Desmond was deeply affected by these unfair practices. In school, he was often told he couldn't achieve as much as White children simply because of his dark skin. But this only fuelled his determination to fight for equality. As a child, he excelled in his studies and was active in sports, showing early signs of leadership and resilience. One day, when he was nine and walking with his mother, he noticed a White priest coming towards them on the path. Normally, he and his

mother would be expected to step off the sidewalk to make room. However, this time, it was the priest who moved and tipped his hat to his mother with great respect. Desmond was amazed, and the memory of that action remained with him. Later he and the priest, who was named Trevor Huddleston, became great friends.

Believing in the power of community, Desmond knew that people working together could overcome any problem. Despite facing discrimination himself, he bravely fought against apartheid's unfair laws. For example, he led peaceful protests such as the 1989 Cape Town peace march, where he and thousands of people walked together to demand an end to apartheid. His strong voice inspired many to hope for a better future.

Empathy and compassion were central to Desmond's life. He dedicated himself to helping others, believing that every person deserved respect, no matter their race or background. He visited hospitals, cared for those who were sick, and assisted those in need, showing that love and kindness could defeat hate and other people's opinions. Desmond embraced the idea of interconnectedness, understanding that we are all linked together like a big family. If one person suffers, then everyone is affected. This belief motivated him to fight for justice and equality, bringing international attention to South Africa's struggles. By standing up against injustice, he aimed to help everyone.

Desmond also recognized how power worked in society. He challenged those who misused their power, knowing that true strength lies in standing up for what

is right, even in tough times. His bravery inspired others to join him in the fight for justice. One of Desmond's most important roles was guiding, as chairperson, the Truth and Reconciliation Commission in 1996. Reconciliation means making peace after a disagreement or conflict. The Commission aimed to help South Africa heal after years of apartheid. People who had suffered or committed crimes during apartheid could come forward to tell their stories. Desmond believed that sharing the truth and forgiving one another were essential for a better future.

Through his leadership, he became an archbishop and a respected church leader. Even amidst violence, he focused on bringing people together and promoting forgiveness. Archbishop Desmond Tutu's life teaches us about empathy, compassion, and humanity. It highlights how a strong community and interconnectedness can help us overcome challenges. Most importantly, it shows that reconciliation and forgiveness can lead to a brighter future for all.

QUESTIONS TO CONSIDER

1. What challenges do you think Desmond Tutu faced while fighting against apartheid? How do you think Desmond Tutu's life changed after he became involved in the struggle for justice?

2. What was the purpose of the Truth and Reconciliation Commission, and how did it help South Africa?

3. How can you show empathy and compassion in your own community?

Illustrator: David Wilkerson

GLOSSARY

Boycott – When people refuse to use or buy something to protest unfair treatment.

Celibacy – When someone decides not to get married or have a close relationship with another person.

Deformity – A part of the body that does not grow or develop as it should, which can affect how it looks or works.

Devotion – A strong love, loyalty, or dedication to a person, cause, or belief.

Discrimination – The unfair treatment of individuals based on their race, gender, or other characteristics.

Empathy – The ability to understand and share how someone else is feeling, as if you were in their shoes.

Endowment – A sum of money that is invested to generate income for a specific purpose, such as scholarships for students.

Endure – To persist and continue through challenges and obstacles.

Equality – The idea that everyone should be treated the same, with the same rights and opportunities, no matter who they are.

Generosity – What it means to be kind, whether by giving money, time, or being willing to help others.

Gospel – The teachings or "good news" of Jesus Christ as recorded in the Bible.

Indigenous – The original Native people who live in a particular land.

Inequality – When people are not treated the same or don't have the same opportunities.

Integrity – What it means to be honest and have strong moral principles.

Justice – Fairness; making sure everyone is treated equally and with respect.

Legacy – Something handed down from the past, like teachings or beliefs.

Martyred – To be killed for one's belief in God.

Miraculous – Something that happens in a way that seems impossible or extraordinary, often considered a sign of divine intervention.

Missionaries – People who travel to various places to teach others about their religion and help communities.

Monastery – A place where monks live and worship.

Monk/Hermit – A holy person who lives alone or with others, often away from society for religious reasons.

Nun – A woman who dedicates her life to God and helps others live out their religious faith.

Ordination – A special Christian service where people are recognized as church leaders.

Pacifist – A person who believes in peace and opposes war or violence.

Pagan – A follower of a polytheistic (belief in many gods) religion, often associated with nature worship.

Patron saint – A saint who is chosen as a special example of faith, protector, or guardian.

Persecution – Mistreatment or harassment based on people's beliefs.

Phonetic – Writing the sounds of speech rather than an alphabet.

Pioneer – Someone who is one of the first to do something.

Prejudice – Having an unfair opinion or attitudes about someone without really knowing them based on their background or appearance.

Racism – Treating someone unfairly just because of their race or where they come from.

Reconciliation – Efforts to help people make peace after a disagreement or conflict.

Reconstruction – The process of rebuilding or restoring something that has been damaged or destroyed.

Resilience – To cope with or recover from setbacks, obstacles or difficulties.

Rhetoric – The art of using language well to persuade or influence others.

Sage – A wise person.

Scholarships – Money given to students to help pay for their education, especially when they don't have enough money to afford it.

Segregation – The practice of keeping people from different races separate, often in an unfair way.

Selflessness – What it means to put the needs and wishes of others before your own.

Slavery – A terrible situation where people are forcibly captured and made to work without pay and treated very cruelly, with no hope of freedom.

Social justice – Making sure everyone is treated fairly and have the same opportunities, no matter who they are.

Solitude – Being alone or isolated from others.

Stereotype – A widely held but simplified and general belief about a group of people.

Theology – The name given to the subject of studying God and things related to faith.

Typhoid – A serious illness caused by bacteria, often spread through contaminated food or water, which makes people sick with fever and stomach problems.

Unwavering – Firm and determined in attitude.

Vow – A serious promise.

ILLUSTRATORS

Amanda Quartey was born and raised in London. At the age of 14 she moved to Ghana and studied art at school and later returned to the UK to study graphic design. Amanda has been working as a professional illustrator since 2020 and is now loving every bit of her illustration career!

As a child, **Amanda Yoshida** dreamed of becoming a picture book illustrator, and she is thrilled to be living her childhood dream as an adult. When she isn't painting or enjoying the gems of Portland, OR, she loves to travel with her beloved son and sidekick, Mo.

Ana Latese is an African American illustrator with a passion to produce beautiful imagery inspired by vibrant tones, magical elements, and joy. She has worked with clients such as the Washington Post, Penguin Random House, Hulu, and Scholastic.

© Élan Vital Visuals

Anastasia Magloire Williams is an award-winning illustrator-author with a lifelong passion for storytelling. Using various styles and vibrant tones, her mission is to elevate unsung histories that reflect the beautiful, diverse world we all share.

Ashley Evans is an illustrator originally from New York City. Her artwork focuses on cute, lively, and bright characters. When she's not drawing you can find her cooking, reading or enjoying time with her loved ones.

Daniela Gamba is a Colombian–American illustrator based in Massachusetts. While studying at Massachusetts College of Art and Design, she discovered her love of digital illustration; focusing on fantasy and sci-fi concept art, she grew up inspired by tales of adventure, and approaches her art-making with the same joy.

David Wilkerson was born in Denver, Colorado. He developed a love for illustration during his high school years. His career began in the animation industry, working as a designer. He's worked on projects for Cartoon Network, PBS Kids, and more.

Born in Winchester, **Jen Khatun** is a published children's book illustrator of Bangladeshi heritage. Her clients include, Lantana, Macmillan Children's Books, OUP, Walker Books, and Penguin. Jen's illustrations encounter a sense of nostaglia, playfulness, and wonder. She now lives by the East Sussex coast with her partner and their dog.

Neda Kazemifar is a New York-based artist and illustrator known for her work on acclaimed titles like *I Survived the Great Molasses Flood, 1919* and *The Refugee*. Discover her portfolio at finifactory.com.

Richy Sanchez Ayala was born and raised in the Dominican Republic. His Caribbean heritage is a big element within his artwork. Richy immigrated to California by way of New York where he pursued his Masters and became an illustrator. Being an immigrant came with challenges but also a keen ability to communicate through pictures.

Samya Zitouni is a Filipino-Moroccan illustrator from Los Angeles. After studying animation at LCAD, she discovered a passion for children's media. She hopes to empower readers through uplifting representation, vibrant illustrations, and championing diverse stories.

© Holland Studios

96